Nathan D. Urner

Never

a hand-book for the uninitated and inexperienced aspirants to refined

society's giddy heights and glittering attainments

Nathan D. Urner

Never
a hand-book for the uninitated and inexperienced aspirants to refined society's
giddy heights and glittering attainments

ISBN/EAN: 9783337390549

Printed in Europe, USA, Canada, Australia, Japan

Cover: Foto ©Andreas Hilbeck / pixelio.de

More available books at **www.hansebooks.com**

Never:

*A Hand-Book for the Unin-
itiated and Inexperienced
Aspirants to Refined So-
ciety's Giddy Heights
and Glittering At-
tainments.*

NEVER

Never:

A Hand-Book for the Uninitiated and Inexperienced Aspirants to Refined Society's Giddy Heights and Glittering Attainments.

"Shoot Folly as it flies,
And catch the manners living as they rise."

Pope.

By MENTOR.

NEW YORK.
COPYRIGHT, 1883, BY
G. W. Carleton & Co., Publishers.

Stereotyped by
SAMUEL STODDER,
42 DEY STREET, N. Y.

Prelude.

*T*HIS *little book is cordially recommended to all parties just hesitating on the plush-padded, gilt-edged threshold of our highest social circles.*

In purely business affairs, it may not be as useful as Hoyle's Games, *or* Locke on the Human Understanding, *but a careful study of its contents cannot but prove the "Open Sesame" to that jealously-guarded realm,—good society,—*

in which you **aspire** **to** circulate freely and shine with becoming luster.

"**It** **is** easier for **a** needle to pass through a camel's **eye**," says Poor Richard, or some one else, "**than for a poor** young **man** **to** enter the mansions of **the** **rich**." And I, **the** author of this code of warnings, **as truly say** unto you, that **a** contemptuous disregard of **the** same will be likely **to** lead you **into** mortification and embarrassment, **if not into** being **incontinently kicked** out of doors.

While intended **chiefly for the** young, not the less may **the old, the** decrepit, and **the** infirm likewise rejoice **in the** possession **of** the rules and prohibitions **herein** contained, **and** hasten to commit **them to** memory.

But the memory is treacherous.

It would, therefore, be well for such persons to carry the Hand Book constantly with them, to be referred to on short notice wherever they may chance to be—in the street-car, in the drawing-room, on the promenade, on the ball-room floor, at table, while visiting, and so on.

In this way the Hand Book will be like the magic ring that pricked the wearer's finger warningly whenever about to yield to an unworthy impulse. Its instructively reiterated " Never" will become, indeed, a blessing—not in disguise, but rather in guardian angel's habiliments.

It will be, in truth, a bosom companion in the

happiest sense of the term, a mutely eloquent monitor of deportment, a still, small voice as to what is in good form and what is not.

Contents.

Never.

I.

Making and Receiving Calls.

NEVER, however formal your visit, neglect to wipe your feet on the door-mat, in lieu of the hall or stair-carpet. A private hall-way is not a stable entrance.

Never bound into the drawing-room unannounced, with your hat, overcoat and overshoes on, nor with your umbrella in your hand, especially if it has been raining hard.

Never, particularly if a comparative stranger, hail your host as "Old Cock," nor grab your hostess's jeweled hand, whether offered to you or not, as if it were a rope's end, and you in danger of drowning. Neither, if other guests are present with whom you have no acquaintance, prance around amongst them, poking them in the ribs, slapping them on the back, etc. True breeding is not synonymous with monkey capers and bar-room manners.

Never be icy or contemptuous ; but never, on the other hand, be fiery or too familiar. Emulate neither the iceberg nor the volcano ; there is a happy medium that can be cultivated to advantage.

Never loll at full length on the sofa, or

bestride a chair with your elbows resting on the back, and the soles of your
boots plainly visible to your *vis-a-vis*.
Sofas are not beds, nor are chairs vault-
ing-horses.

Never, even when sitting in your chair,
tilt it far back, with your heels resting
on the mantel-piece, and your back to
the rest of the company present. Are
you a gentleman or an orang-outang?

Never, either, keep twisting and squirm-
ing about in your chair as if sitting on a
hornet's nest, nor keep crossing and re-
crossing the legs every second and a
half, nor carve your initials on the fur-
niture with your penknife. St. Vitus'
dance is one thing, dignified repose another.

Never, in being introduced to a lady, make a pun on her name, if it is a homely one, or jokingly allude to rouge-pots and whited sepulchers, if she is no longer young, with an air of having resorted to preservative aids. Illogical but intuitive, the feminine mind is swift to imagine and resent an innuendo where perhaps none was intended.

Never, if the lady be young but homely, at once patronizingly remark that, after all, handsome is as handsome does, and you have even known the dowdiest and most unattractive girls make good matches through tact and perseverance. However laudable your intention, there may be a muscular brother inconveniently in the background.

Never attempt to sing or play, even though pressed to do so, if you are absolutely ignorant of both vocal and instrumental music. Effects might, indeed, be produced, but would they be desirable?

Never be so self-conscious as to fancy yourself a cave-bear and other people but field-mice. "True politeness will betray no hoggishness," as 'an ancient writer has sagely observed.

Never, especially with your superiors, buttonhole people, or shake your fist in their faces, or pound them in the ribs when you have occasion to address them. This is more appropriate to a horse auction than a drawing-room, and is in violation of good form.

Never lean across one person with your

hands on his knees and your back-hair in his face, to talk to another.

Never bawl out at the top of your lungs, or try to monopolize all the talk ; you are neither in the stock exchange nor a cattle yard.

Never, if bald and warm, mop and rub up your head, ears and neck with your handkerchief. A reception or drawing-room is not a barber-shop.

Never intrude your maladies upon the general conversation. People cannot be so much interested in your bunions or backache as you are.

Never violently abuse people who may overhear you, nor be bitingly witty at another's expense.

Never interrupt the general conversation

by reading long-winded newspaper reports aloud.

Never contemptuously criticise the furni-
ture, the pictures, or the wall-paper as
being cheap and mean. This is but a
scurvy return for the hospitality you are
enjoying.

Never chew tobacco, or smoke a pipe at
receptions. If you must do the one or
the other, be sure to use the cuspidor ;
but it is safer to let up on tobacco until
out-of-doors, or in your own room.

Never calumniate people, or give a false
coloring to your statements. In other
words, don't lie any more than you can
help. Be diplomatic.

Never, above all, fail in tact. For instance, don't say that the room is as

cold as a barn, even if you think so. Tact and fact may not always go hand-in-hand.

Never interrupt or contradict overbearingly, or with a sort of snort. Either of these faults is directly opposed to the canons of good society.

Never be explosive or pugnacious, accompanying your side of an argument with roaring explosives and furious gesticulations. A lady's parlor is not a bear-garden.

Never, on the other hand, be cowering and sniveling, as though desirous of some one to kick you as a boon. In deportment, the demeanor of the rabbit is no more to be emulated than that of the famished wolf.

Never, in the midst of a discussion upon solemn topics, retail antediluvian jokes, and then ha, ha! boisterously at them when no one else can see anything to laugh at. In fine, don't be an unmitigated bore.

Never gape, yawn, "heigh ho," or stamp your feet disapprovingly, when others are talking. This is blighting, if not fairly irritating.

Never be unduly "stuck up." Because you are yourself is no reason why you are William H. Vanderbilt or George Francis Train.

Never sulk and growl under your breath, like a bear with a sore head, because you fancy yourself neglected. Brighten up, and even snicker, rather than adopt

this gloomy course.   Moroseness is dis-
piriting.

Never even murder a persistent bore
until you get outside. To send for the
police might cause an inconvenience.

Never, if playing cards with ladies, spit on
your hands when dealing, or mark the
bowers and aces with pencil-marks or
knife-punctures. Englishmen would be
especially horrified at such a proceed-
ing.

Never rave, tear your hair, or swear there
has been cheating all around, even if you
have lost ten cents on the game. Either
bear your losses with equanimity, or
never gamble.

Never treat aged and venerable persons
like budding hoodlums, or make riotous

fun of their wrinkles or their bald heads. You may be old yourself, some time, if not assassinated for your bad manners.

Never neglect to give precedence to ladies, both on entering and quitting a room. A brutal disregard of this injunction might cause you to be led out by the ear.

Never, as hostess, insist that a casual caller shall send for his trunk and stay a week or two.

Never, as host, ask him hilariously if he is well over his last drunk, and getting primed for another. This is not in good taste.

Never hurry your departure, as if your legs were sticks and your body a sky-rocket.

Never, on the other hand, tarry from, say, four in the afternoon till three in the morning. A light, flying visit is one thing, taking root another.

II.

At Breakfast.

NEVER descend to the breakfast-room without having washed your face and brushed your hair. Cleanliness is a part of good breeding.

Never appear at breakfast, even in sultry weather, without your coat, waistcoat, collar and necktie. Are you a gentleman or a Hottentot?

Never, even in winter, take your seat at the table in your top-boots, with your overcoat buttoned to the chin, and with a sealskin cap drawn down to your eye-

brows.   But if you are breakfasting in
Franz Josef's Land, this warning may
be disregarded.

Never fail to help the ladies first, before
gorging every edible in sight.   You will
thus cultivate a reputation for self-abne-
gation that may stand you in stead.

Never, if a guest, inspect the butter suspi-
ciously, smelling and tasting it, and then
say, " Pretty good butter—what there
is of it!"   Never, having perceived
your blunder, hasten to rectify it by
calling out, " Ay, and plenty of it, too—
such as it is! Ha, ha, ha!"   Better ab-
stain from criticism altogether, since
nothing is costing you anything.

Never insist on starting this meal with
soup. *Cazuela*, or breakfast soup, is a

Spanish-American custom that has not yet been imported.

Never, before expressing your preference for tea or coffee, ask your hostess which she would recommend as the least poisonous? She might not consider the insinuation as complimentary to herself.

Never dispose of eggs by biting off the small end, throwing the head far back, and noisily sucking them out of the shells. A spoon, or even a fork, is preferable. Besides you might encounter a bad one when too late.

Never wipe your nose on your napkin, or use it in dusting off your boots on rising. Napkins have their legitimate uses, handkerchiefs theirs.

Never, on finishing with your napkin,

fastidiously fold it away in its ring, nor carelessly hang it on the chandelier. Use judgment in little things.

Never cool your tea or coffee by pouring it back and forth from cup to saucer and from saucer to cup in a high arching torrent, after the manner of a diamond-fastened bar-tender with a cocktail or julep. There's a time and place for everything.

Never suck your knife contemplatively, and then dive it in the butter-dish. This is wholly indefensible.

Never use the butter-knife in besmearing and plastering your bread with butter an inch thick. Better tear up the bread in small chunks, and sop up the butter with it.

Never cut meat with your teaspoon, sip tea from a fork, or painfully suggest sword-swallowing by eating with your knife. Try to appear civilized.

Never convey the impression that you are shoveling food down an excavation rather than eating it. Cultivated people eat, barbarians engulf.

Never smack the lips and roll the eyes while masticating, accompanying the operation with such expressions as, "Oh, golly, but that's good!" "Aha, that touches the spot!" Give your neighbors a show.

Never reach far over the table with both hands for a coveted morsel. Ask for it, call a servant, or circulate around the table behind the other breakfasters' chairs.

Never shake your fist at the waiters, or swear at them in loud and imperious tones. This is not the best form even in a restaurant.

Never pounce on a particular morsel, intended for an invalid, like a hawk on a June-bug. First, say to yourself reflectively, " Am I in a private breakfast-room or a barn ?"

Never try to dispose of beefsteak, peach-jam and coffee at the same mouthful. Failure, complete and ignominious, will be the result.

Never, if at a tenth-rate boarding-house, insist upon having broiled game. In the bright lexicon of the boarding-house there's no such word as quail.

Never, unless you are John L. Sullivan,

indicate your irritation by upsetting the table, or shying muffins at the landlord. Equability of temper and a good appetite should go hand in hand.

Never fail in urbanity with those around you. Loud squabbling, fighting with the feet under the table, and open rivalry for the smiles of a pretty waitress are altogether alien to the higher culture.

Never make a pretense, on quitting the table, of mistaking the napkin for your handkerchief. This is an old, old dodge.

Never stretch yourself, gulch, gape and yawp on rising. You should have finished all that in bed.

Never refer to the meal you have disposed of under the generic name of " hash."

The commonness of this fault does not excuse it.

Never fail in bowing gracefully when abandoning the table, and, in lighting your cigar, never strike a match on your hostess's back. Be keenly observant of your well-bred neighbors, and you will at last learn to avoid these little breaches of etiquette that are so painstakingly enumerated for your cultivation.

III.

At Luncheon.

NEVER become notorious as that most unfortunate and reprehensible of mortals —the Lunch Fiend. If at a *pseudo* free-lunch, drink something at the bar first, if only a glass of water.

Never gorge at a luncheon, as if there were never to be a dinner-hour. A gentleman is never supposed to be ravenous.

Never indiscriminately mix your liquors at this hour. A little whisky or brandy as an appetizer, with not more than four varieties of wine while eating, and topping off with a few mugs of beer, should be quite satisfying.

Never, if at a fashionable collation, discuss business, politics or abstruse scientific problems with the fair creatures present. Sink the shop, if only for ten minutes.

Never jocosely give wrong names to well-known dishes before you. To denominate breaded cutlets " fried horse," cold corned beef " mule-meat," and sliced tongue " larded elephants' ears," may be humorous, but hardly in keeping with the light festivities of the occasion.

Never, if ignorant of certain dishes, attempt to denominate them at all. If found palatable, eat and ask no questions.

Never fail to let a lady sip out of your glass, if she entreats you to that effect. You can secretly throw away the contents afterward, but a direct insult was not embodied in the request.

Never refuse to hold a lady's saucer of ice-cream for her, and feed her with a spoon, at her earnest request. This betrays a guileless trust in you that should be esteemed as complimentary.

Never be detected in surreptitiously stuffing your pockets with raisins, fruit-cake and peanuts. It will not be so much the theft as the detection that will cause the honest blush to mantle in your virile cheek.

Never attract a lady's attention by playfully signaling her across the table with

melon-rinds or banana-peel. To trun-
dle a napkin-ring straight over into her
lap were in better taste.

Never regale the company with detailed
descriptions of similar repasts that you
have enjoyed in Pekin, but where puppy-
dog roasts, rat-pie and sharks' fins were
the most appetizing features. Though
roars of laughter reward your recital,
you are not now in the antipodes.

Never give in in a contest over a favorite
turkey-bone with a spoiled child of the
family. Even if his howls shatter the
frescoes, never forget that you are his
senior, hence his superior.

Never feed your hostess's favorite cat or
lap-dog at the lunch-table, by setting
the pretty creature on your shoulder,
and tossing up scraps to him between

your own mouthfuls.   This may be art-
less, but is not in the' best taste.

Never neglect to quit the table after all
the other guests have retired.   To con-
tinue gorging and guzzling in solitary
state is to make a show of yourself to
the menials.

Never fail, when you have at last fully
decided to give the repast a rest, to
quit the room easily, though with a dignified air.   To dance away with a hop,
skip and a jump, while trolling out "a
careless, careless tavern-catch," or with
painful grimaces, while convulsively
clutching the pit of the stomach with
both hands, is to hint a reflection upon
the hospitality you have enjoyed.   This
might subject you to unflattering comment.

IV.

At Dinner.

NEVER forget that this is the repast *par excellence.*

Never, as an invited guest, be more than two hours late. Your host and hostess, as well as the other guests, may have starved themselves for a fortnight for this particular gorge.

Never, in handing in a lady, struggle desperately to pass through the dining-room dooway two abreast, if said aperture admits but one at a time sidewise. Even if it break your proud heart, give the lady precedence always.

Never sit six feet off from the table, nor
yet so crunched up against it as to
cause you indescribable torture. Well
within feeding distance, with ample
elbow-room for knife-and-fork play, is
your safest rule.

Never tuck your napkin all around under
your collar-band, nor make a child's bib
of it. You are not in a barber's chair
nor at a baby-farm.

Never suck up your soup with a straw,
nor, with your elbows on the table and
the plate-rim at your lips, drink it down
with happy gurgles and impetuous haste.
Go for it with a spoon for all you are
worth. Never ask for more than a
fourth service of soup.

Never bury your nose in your plate, while

using your knife, **fork** and spoon **at the same** time, after the manner **of** Chinese chop-sticks. **Maintain as** erect an attitude as **you can** without endangering **your** spinal column, though **not** as if you **had** swallowed **a poker.**

Never exhibit **surprise or irritation,** should you **overturn** your soup **in your lap.** Rise majestically, **and** while the **waiter is wiping it** off, calmly declare that **you** were **born** under a lucky **star, since not a drop** has spattered your clothes.

Never snap **off** your bread **in enormous** chunks, **to be** filtered and washed down **by** gravy **or** wine. Rather than this, crumb **it** off **into** pellets, **to be** skillfully tossed **into the** mouth **as** occasion **may** demand.

Never ram your knife more than half-way down your throat. Hack with your knife, claw up with your fork ; that is what they're made for. Never take up a great meat-slice on your fork, and then leisurely nibble around the corners, making steady inroads till your teeth strike silver. This is a method rigidly interdicted among the highest circles.

Never eat fish with a spoon, if the silver butter-knife can be appropriated for that purpose.

Never eat as if you had bet high on getting away with the entire banquet in six minutes and a half. This may be complimentary to the viands, but is somewhat vulgar.

Never, when the champagne begins to
circulate, snatch the bottle from the
waiter's hand, hang on to the nozzle,
tilt up the butt, and ingurgitate for dear
life, while approvingly patting your
stomach with your disengaged hand.
This is little short of an enormity.

Never devour spinach with a mustard-
spoon, spear beans with a wooden tooth-
pick, or mistake the gravy for another
course of soup. Take your cue from
such of your neighbors as appear least
like hogs.

Never clean up and polish off your plate,
as if it were a magnifying lens, before
sending it for a second installment.
There are scullions in the kitchen, or
ought to be.

Never spit back rejected morsels on your
plate, nor toss fruit-stones under the
table, nor hide fish-bones under the
ornamental center-pieces. An obdurate
piece of gristle should be bolted at all
hazards, fruit-stones may be dexterously
transferred to your neighbor's plate, and
fish-bones may be cleverly utilized as a
garniture for the salt-cellars and butter-
plates.

Never hurry matters when fully half-
gorged, when there is a ringing in your
ears, and things begin to swim before
your eyes. These are warnings to taper
off slowly, in preparation for dessert.

Never adhere wholly to champagne
throughout the repast. A few glasses
of claret as between-drinks, with now

and then a quencher of brown sherry, afford an agreeable variety.

Never forget to occasionally look after the lady under your care. She may, moreover, be useful in passing you dishes during the temporary vanishings of the servant.

Never attempt a flirtation, or even a sustained conversation, during the repast. Gastronomy is a noble but jealous mistress, who permits no division of your allegiance.

Never, when dessert is served, wade into the jellies and riot amid the tarts and cakes as if you were just getting up your wind for a fresh onslaught. Be moderate.

Never ask for a soup-plate of ice-cream.

It is better form to have your saucer replenished again and again.

Never talk when your mouth is fairly crammed, nor in a smothered, wheezy tone of voice. It is more dignified to bow blandly, point to your mouth in explanation of your predicament, and wag your head.

Never be so pre-occupied with drinking as not to be on the look-out for the lady under your care. She has a right to her share of the liquids.

Never be embarrassed. Retain your self-possession if you are choking.

Never forget your own wants under any circumstances. Remember that self-respect is as much of a virtue as respect for others.

Never be self-conscious. Guzzle quietly, and let others take care of themselves.

Never, on the other hand, push self-depreciation to the wall. Never lose sight of the fact that, while you are a gentleman, you are also an American sovereign feasting at some one else's expense. All sovereigns do that.

Never, if called upon for a toast, be afraid to pledge yourself. It you don't blow your own trumpet, who will blow it for you ?

Never use your fork for a tooth-pick, nor the edge of the table-cloth for a napkin. Summon a servant, and make known your wants in imperious, stentorian tones.

Never lounge back in your chair, and

request the waiter to pour wine down your throat, if too unsteady to longer hold a glass. This is apt to be noticeable.

Never rest both elbows on the table, while shuffling your feet nervously underneath it, and trying to steer one more glass to your lips. If paralysis threatens, request to be led out.

Never lose your temper. "When a man has well-dined," says an old playwright, "he should feel in a good humor with all the world."

Never fail to rise when the ladies are leaving the table, and to remain standing somehow, no matter how unsteadily, until the last petticoat has disappeared. Then, your duty having been performed,

you can roll under the table, if you want
to, or see-saw back to your anchorage,
and see if you can hold any more wine.
Never drink too much wine. True, there
are a variety of opinions as to how
much is too much; but be prudent, be
resolved, never make an exhibition of
yourself, at least *try* to knock off before
being paralyzed, and be happy.
Never, however, yield to the jocular pro-
pensities of your brother guests. Should
they prop you in a corner of the room,
with your hair drawn over your eyes
and a lamplighter in your mouth for a
cigar, and then jocosely vociferate
" Speech ! speech !" heroically reach for
the nearest bottle, back with your head,
and guzzle away. A philosopher, a

real gentleman, will never be laughed down, sneered under, or rubbed out.

Never, if called on for a speech in a complimentary way, however, make a rostrum of the table at which you have dined. Rather essay your own chair. the window-sill, or even the mantelpiece.

Never fail in courtesy, even when grossly intoxicated. Apologize, even if you have slumbered on your neighbor's shoulder, and murmur your excuses even while disappearing under the table. An exponent of high breeding never forgets to be a gentleman under the most adverse circumstances.

Never whistle, sing ditties, or jeer irrelevantly while another guest is responding

to a popular toast. You surely should
not wish to monopolize the entire
oratorical effects of the occasion ; and,
moreover, boorish interruption is always
in equivocal form.

V.

While Walking.

NEVER fail to maintain a firm but easy
attitude. The willow, not the light-
ning-rod, will afford you the best sug-
gestions.

Never walk over people, but around them.
Men and women are not stepping-stones
or door-mats, save to monarchs and
rich corporations.

Never neglect to apologize if you stamp
on a man's corns, or jostle him into an
excavation.

Never howl with laughter at any pecu-

liarity of aspect, manner **or** dress.   Be
a gentleman always.

Never crush and shoulder your way
through groups **of** ladies at shop-win-
dows, with your **cane** menacingly twirled
aloft, shillelah-fashion.   Analogy **be-**
tween **a** fashionable promenade and
Donnybrook Fair is wholly apocryphal.

Never smoke **in** the street, unless **you can**
afford a good article.   Chinese cigar-
ettes, **long** nines, **and** black cutty pipes
are decidedly **in** bad form.

Never, **if you** must **smoke,** whiffle your
smoke **in others'** faces, or playfully burn
them **in** the back of the neck, or ask **a**
lady **for a** light.   Walter Raleigh, the
father **of** tobacco-using, **even** carried his
own cuspidor.

Never munch nuts or gorge fruits in public. A lady or gentleman on the afternoon promenade, with a peeled pineapple in one hand, a huge slice of watermelon in the other, and the jaws industriously working, is not an edifying spectacle.

Never forget, if with a lady, that she is under your protection, not you under hers.

Never rush her past an oyster-saloon at a run, or wildly distract her attention from a confectioner's window. As a woman, she has her privileges.

Never drag her, pell-mell, with you through a mob of fighting roughs.

Never forget to be kind, even while feigning deafness to all insinuations as to refreshment. " Kindness iz an instinkt," says Josh Billings, " while politeness iz only an art."

Never neglect to give her at least a portion of your umbrella, when escorting her through the rain. If it should rain cats and dogs, as the saying goes, an adjournment beneath an awning, or front-stoop, might be deemed advisable.

Never, if walking with a tramp, introduce him to every acquaintance you chance to meet. It is a free country, but the line must be drawn somewhere.

Never, if you have occasion to address a strange lady, scrape, cringe and wriggle before her in an agony of politeness. To raise your hat gravely, place your hand on your heart, and yield her a low, sweeping obeisance, with your shoulders shrugged considerably higher than your ears, is sufficient. You are not supposed to be a Corean ambassador in the presence of Jay Gould.

Never address questions to strangers indiscriminately, especially as to their secret and private affairs. Communicativeness is not a necessary outcome of a total lack of sodality.

Never, even in questioning a policeman, fan him with his own club, note down his number, and ask him if he has yet got the hair off his teeth. Though in livery, he may yet be above the brute creation.

Never ask questions at all, but consult this Hand Book.

Never, if suddenly confronted on the promenade by a hostile acquaintance, accept his proposition to fight him in the gutter for a pot of beer. You are not a Prize Fighter.

Never forget to pick up a lady's handkerchief, if she lets it fall by accident ; not with effusive familiarity, but daintily on the end of your cane or umbrella. Common civility is one of the cardinal points of good breeding.

Never pick it up at all, if she drops it purposely. You needn't set your foot on it, or scowl at her ; but coquetry is one of the vices deserving of silent reproof.

Never pick up anything that even your companion may drop, unless he should be very drunk. You may pick him up also, if he should drop.

Never, even if in haste, rush through a crowded thoroughfare at a breakneck gait, with your hair flying, your necktie over your ears, and shouting " Clear the track !" at every jump. Hire a cab, or obtain roller-skates. Repose of manner should never be sacrificed to emotional insanity.

Never pose on street corners, attitudinize before show-case mirrors, or whistle an opera bouffe air while watching a funeral cortege.

Never, if with a lady, ask her to wait for you on the curb while you step into an adjacent bar-room to see a man. The ruse is a transparent one, and, moreover, she may be thirsty herself.

Never hilariously address a stranger with an obvious defect of vision as " Squinty," nor ask another how many barrels of whisky it has taken to paint his nose. Such familiarities may possibly be resented.

Never, on the other hand, be so over-civil as to be mistaken for a dancing master or a bunco-steerer.

Never forget that a gentleman is a gentleman everywhere. Even McGilder was occasionally taken for one.

Never have your shoes polished in the middle of the sidewalk while hanging on to an awning-beam for support. It may create the impression that all the polish you have is upon your shoes.

VI.

In the Use of Language.

Never cease trying to make yourself understood. Learn to read and write before you are of age.

Never pronounce with your teeth clenched, through the nose, or by ripping up the sounds laboriously from the pit of the stomach. Speak gently, but with clarion-like distinctness.

Never squeal like a rat, grunt like a pig, or roar like a bull. Cultivate a pleasing voice.

Never smother your meaning out of sight

with slang. "Soup should be seasoned, not red-hot," says an old writer.

Never swear, anathematize, or fairly drip with profanity, especially in the presence of delicate ladies and small children. Undue emphasis often defeats itself.

Never indicate a mere passing surprise by such expressions as "Holy smoke!" "Gosh almighty!" "I'm teetotally dashed!" and the like. A mere lifting of the eyebrows, a convulsive gasp, or a wild, staggered look, while smiting the forehead with the fist, will be demonstrative enough.

Never say *sir* to a bootblack and *old chap* to a minister of the gospel in the same breath. Exercise tact.

Never say " No, mum " or "Yessum," in

addressing a lady, or "Not much, old hoss," or "yezzur," in speaking to a gentleman, even if these chance to be your parents or near relatives. "No, dad," "Yes, mommy," "No, granny," "Yes, nunksy," and so on, are more affectionate.

Never address a young lady as *Jen.*, *Mol.*, *Pol.*, *Bet.*, *Suke.*, or by any other abbreviation of her given name. *Miss So-and-so*, or plain *miss*, is in better form.

Never address a young married lady as *old girl*, even if you were intimate with her before her marriage. Her husband may not apprehend your facetiousness.

Never mispronounce. Never say *purtect* for *protect*, *yer* for *you*, *tater* for *potato*, *this 'ere* for *this here*, *tommytoes* for *toma-*

toes, voilent for *violent, aborgoyne* for *aborigine,* or *busted* for *bursted.* " Take her up tenderly, lift her with care."

Never say *kin* for *can, they'se* for *they're, feller* for *fellow,* **gal** for **girl,** *wuz* for *was,* **whar** for *where,* **thar** for *there, har* for *hair,* **hev** for *have, wull* for *will, cud* for *could,* nor **wud** for *would.* Never imagine that ignoramuses only fall into these errors. The greatest scholars in the world have been known to fairly revel in them when suffering from *delirium tremens,* or otherwise off their guard.

Never forget that *duty* rhymes with *beauty,* not with *booty,* and that *morn* doesn't rhyme with *dawn* at all—poetasters to the contrary notwithstanding. Even a gentleman of the world will not wholly despise the soft demands of rhythm.

Never say *idear* for *idea*, nor *wahm* for *warm*. The addition of the *r* in the one case is as indefensible as its omission in the other.

Never say *pants* for *trousers*, *vest* for *waistcoat*, *boiled rag* for *shirt*, nor *trotter cases* for *boots* and *shoes*. As a sole alternative, let your language be choice to fastidiousness.

Never allude to a *cuss*, meaning a *man*. Even *pure cussedness* for *sheer contrariety* is becoming the property of the common herd.

Never say "the old woman," alluding to your wife. Is marriage of necessity the grave of respect?

Never speak of your father as "the governor," "the old man," "the money-bag," and the like. Perhaps, he is a very good sort of person.

Never say *castor* for hat, nor *gun-boats* for *overshoes*, nor *duds* for *clothes* in general. A multiplication of these synonyms may be creditable to the invention, but is apt to be confusing.

Never fear to say you are *sick*, if you are so. Englishmen are *h'ill*, and Frenchmen are at liberty to be *indisposé*. We never say "an ill room," or "an indisposed bed," but "a sick room" or "a sick bed," as the case may be.

Never ask if the railroad has come in, but if the train has come in. The track can no more come and go than can the station itself.

Never pile on the adjectives. A painting may be meritorious without being " stunning ;" a handsome wall-paper is not necessarily " excruciating ; " and you should hardly · call a choice dish of ham and eggs "divine." Let not your enthusiasm overleap itself.

Never say *naw, nixy, not by a blamed sight,* nor *nary a time,* for pure and simple *no.* Let the negative be swift, clear and decisive, even in declining a drink.

Never say *yis, yaw* nor *ya-as,* for *yes,* unless you swear by the shamrock, the Bologna sausage, or the roast beef of old England.

Never say that you believe you'll take root or come to anchor, when you intend sitting down, nor say "squattyvous " to a friend in requesting him to take a seat.

Never, if you must use slang, fail to make a judicious choice of it. Who was it said, " Let me but make the slang of a people, and he who will make their laws?" But no matter; since there is plenty of it ready-made. Never attempt to add thereto, but be content to separate the wheat from the chaff, the fine gold from the dross.   .

Never speak of a bar-room as "a h'istery," "a whisky ranch," "a rum-hole," or "a jig-water dispensary." Plain old Anglo-Saxon "gin-mill" must hold its own against the innovations of storming time.

Never, in speaking confidentially to a

young lady of her father's tippling habits, refer to him as " an old soaker," "a rum-head," "a guzzler," "a perambulating beer-keg," or "a happy-go-lucky old swill-tub." Far better to slur matters gently by recommending an inebriate asylum, or suggesting that the old gentleman be locked up with a whisky-barrel, with a fair chance of his drinking himself to death.

Never, at social gatherings, speak of elderly ladies as " old hens," nor of the children of the house as " kids." But a careful study of the very best society will soon make these pitfalls apparent to you.

Never, in entreating a young lady to sing, ask her if she can't chirp or twitter a bit.

Never, after she has sung, and with obvious effort, playfully suggest that she has a bellows to mend. To gaze into her eyes lingeringly, and whisper that you did not mean to knock her endwise, would be more considerate and soothing.

Never say, *smeller*, *horn*, *bugle*, or *snoot* for *nose.* Never say *peepers* for *eyes*, *potato-trap* for *mouth*, nor *bread-basket* for *stomach*, at least not in the very highest circles. *Olfactor*, *optics* and *paunch* are a choice disguise for the Queen's English, if that is the end in view.

Never say that a man was "howling mad" or "jumping crazy," meaning that he was very angry, when you have such tempting morsels as "hopping mad," "frothing at the mouth," "mad as a hatter," and "crazy as a bedbug" at your disposal.

Never say, "Well, I should smile," meaning that you assent to something said or proposed, when honest old "You can bet your boots I will" is coyly nestling near at hand, craving a caress.

Never ask, "How in ——— am I going to do it?" when silvery "Do it youself, and be blowed!" may lend a mingled suavity and conciseness to the situation.

Never say, "busted in the snoot" for "thumped in the proboscis." This is wholly inexcusable.

Never say "I *seed*" for "I *saw*," "I *heerd*" for "I *heard*," or "I *thunk*" for "I *thought*." Notwithstanding that these gross mistakes may be in vogue among highly-educated men, newspaper editors and professional linguists, erect a standard of your own rather than follow in their unworthy lead.

Never say, " Him an' me is goin' to the circus," when " He and I *are* going to the circus" is meant. This scarcely perceptible inaccuracy brings many a conscientious student to grief.

Never say, " They is well, but I are not." Painstaking discernment will enable you to make the correction.

Never say " Between you and I and the pump-handle," meaning " Between you and me."

Never speak of dinner as " grub," " hash " or " trough-time,"nor refer to the dessert as " an after-clap."

Never, if you have been on a spree, allude to it as a " boose," a " toot," a " twist," a " rolling big drunk," a " bust," or a "bump," when strong, sensible " budge," " bender " and " jamboree " are peeping wistfully from the catalogue.

Never proclaim that you are "chocked to the throat," meaning simply that you have dined plentifully.

Never be afraid to call a spade a "spade," even if you have bet on hearts or dia-monds.

Never, if intoxicated, say that you are " weaving the winding way," " slopping over," " six sheets in the wind," or "screwed." The latter is wholly British, and not yet adopted with us.

Never repeat worn-out saws and proverbs,

such as " It's a long turn that makes no lane," " It's an ill wind that blows your hat off," and the like. Better use your own invention than harp forever on a moldered string.

Never, moreover, repeat much-used quotations, no matter how celebrated they may once have been. "We have met the enemy and we are theirs," and "Whoever undertakes to shoot down the American flag, haul him on the spot," may be patriotic, but they weary, they weary!

Never call a pretender a " cad," when either "fraud" or "dead-beat" can safely give odds to the importation.

Never allude to your time-piece as a "cracker," a "turnip" or a "ticker," nor

to your hands as " mawlies," " fins " or
"flippers," nor to your fingers as
" digits." The use of any one of these
slang terms indicates a want of higher
culture.

Never, in referring to an enemy, say that
you will " put a head on him bigger
than a bushel-basket," merely meaning
that you will punch him.

Never say "peart" for clever

Never say *oncommon* for *uncommon*, nor
comment upon a delicacy by saying
that it is "licking good."

Never say, in commenting upon a lady's
appearance, that she looked like a
"fright," like a "frump," or like " a
bundle of bones tied up with rags."
You have " dowdy" and "scarecrow"
to fall back on.

Never wish aloud that a man may be
hanged, drawn and quartered, simply
because he owes you a dollar and a
quarter. Fiendish resentment is not
one of the shining characteristics of·a
true gentleman.

Never, when in doubt as to any particular
form of expression, fail to consult this
Hand Book. It is the one faithful
lamp by which your steps may be
guided.

VII.

Dress and Personal Habits.

NEVER forget to wash yourself and brush your hair (if you have any) before quitting your room in the morning. To make your toilet at the kitchen sink, or even at a convenient fire-plug, is to set the canons of good society at naught.

Never re-appear in the morning with a dirty shirt, a crushed hat, and with your necktie under your ear. This might convey the impression that you had gone to bed in your clothes.

Never be filthy in anything. Cleanliness

is a virtue that even a recognized gentleman cannot afford to hold in contempt.

Never appear in other than subdued colors, for the most part. " Give me plain red and yellow," said the negro minister, in his advice to his flock on the vanities of dress.

Never wear anything over-dainty. Never —of course, we are now addressing the male reader, for whom this invaluable Hand Book is chiefly designed—wear anything that the gentler sex have made exclusively their own. To appear in public with a nosegay in lieu of a throat-stud, or even with a sunflower at the waist, would be likely to excite remark.

Never wear check-shirts, children's dickies, nor 'longshoremen's jumpers. An immaculate shirt-front with a clean collar to match, is always *en règle.*

Never wear full evening dress in the early morning, especially if you intend working in the garden, or whitewashing the back fence, before going down town.

Never wear dancing pumps in rainy or snowy weather, or arctics if it is warm and fine. But long-continued observation will finally enable you to discriminate for yourself in these minor matters.

Never appear among ladies with your boots covered with mud, and your whole person suggestive of having been rolled in the gutter. If you haven't a servant or wife to clean you up, undertake the task yourself, however distasteful.

Never wear your hat tilted far over your
nose, with a cigar meeting its brim at a
rising angle of forty-five degrees from
your lips.   The Volunteer Fire Depart-
ment, though once the arbiter of manly
deportment, is a thing of the past.

Never wear pinchbeck jewelry, loud breast-
pins, nor steel, silver or washed-gold
watch-guards.   Secret-society regalia,
conspicuously worn, and multitudinous
finger-rings are also in questionable
taste.

Never walk with a high-and-mighty stud-
horse gait, nor yet slouch and slink
along as if you had robbed a hen-roost,
nor yet with a bounding hoop-la sort of
prance, like a clown in the circus-ring.
Never, either, walk bow-legged or club-

footed, if you can help it. Cultivate a grand, regal, easy and flowing carriage, but without swagger or bombast.

Never walk, especially if in haste, with your arms folded, nor with your hands in your coat-tail pockets.

Never improvise tooth-picks out of fence splints, and then chew them industriously in public. Tobacco and chewing-gum still assert their claims.

Never expectorate all around you at every step you take, without an instant's intermission. If you are troubled with bronchitis, remain at home. If the same old drunk persistently lingers, try a B. and S., or a gin fizz, according to your judgment.

Never whistle like a locomotive, nor at-

tempt a Tyrolese *jodel,* while walking
with a lady or ladies on a fashionable
promenade.

Never whittle sticks, play on a jewsharp,
or essay to catch flies on window-panes
in public. Such recreations, innocent
in themselves, should only be pursued
in the privacy of one's own apartment.

Never permit the quality or cut of your
wearing-apparel to deteriorate, if you
have to live on pork and beans to keep
up your end in this regard. "Never
retrench in your wardrobe expenses,
whatever you do," said old Samuel
Pepys. "All the world knows how you
appear, but no one need know how you
live." A frequent change of residence
might serve to disconcert the tailors,
should they prove troublesome.

Never allow your shoes to run down at the heel, nor out at the toes. Nothing is more incongruous than a fine gentleman, in other respects quite the swell, with his foot-leather burst out around the instep, his stocking heels wabbling up and down at every jump, and his bare toes courting the public gaze.

Never hiccough or sneeze without intermission, unless greatly inebriated. In this dilemma, lose no time in drinking yourself sober, or in seeking temporary retirement, if only on a park-bench.

Never let your lower lip hang down on your breast, like a motherless calf's. "Put up or shut up," says the Coptic proverb.

Never, on the other hand, screw up your

lips under your nose, as though constantly subjected to an overpowering
odor. Even a prevailing ecstatic, attar-
of-roses haunted expression is in preferable form to.this.

Never fail to keep your nose clean. If
you have no handkerchief, use your
coat-tail.

Never cultivate a broad, teeth-husking
smile, unless your ivories are in good
order. Tobacco-stained fangs are at an
especial disadvantage in this form.

Never fail to cleanse the teeth at least
once a week. A tooth-brush is best.

Never wear your hat in church, in a
boudoir, nor at a marriage or burial
service ; never, on the other hand, take
it off when overtaken by a blizzard or a

cyclone. If neither the blizzard nor the cyclone does that much for you, you may consider yourself fortunate.

Never doff your hat nor make your bow indiscriminately. A Cyrus Field, for instance, would be justified in expecting greater courtesy than would be accorded to a Jesse James ; though, if cornered by one of the latter type on his own stamping-ground, it would doubtless be well not to slight him too conspicuously. . Be diplomatic.

Never fail to cultivate an off-hand judgment of men and women who are strangers to you. A man with a head like a monkey's is not necessarily a savant ; nor are putty-like faces, with idiotic lips and China-blue eyes, in women, necessarily Elizabeth Cady Stantonesque in intellectual scope and oratorical brilliancy. You would scarcely mistake Red Leary for Herbert Spencer.

Never carry a lighted cigar into a millinery store or powder-magazine.

Never be over servile to good clothes for themselves alone. The professional thief who lost his life in a double tragedy in Sixth avenue not long ago, was one of the best dressed men in New York.

Never, on the other hand venture to indiscriminately despise slovenly dress in men or women. Lady Burdette-Coutts is said to occasionally slouch around London like a charwoman just for the fun of the thing; good old Steve Girard was wont to dress like a music-master in distress; and some greasy, old, garlic-smelling tatterdemalion at your elbow may be one of the most successful pawnbrokers of the Hebraic persuasion.

Never burst, without notice, into any one's private apartment like a shot out of a gun. Even your excuse that you want to borrow your car-fare may not be mollifying, and people have nerves.

Never keep gnawing your mustache, twisting your whiskers into fantastic braids, nor making your hat wag about on your head through muscular contraction of the scalp.

Never crackle your knuckles with sharp reports, grit your teeth, heave deep, wheezing sighs, nor keep running your fingers through your hair till it stands up like a brush-heap. If you imagine one or all of these feats to be uniquely interesting, hire out to a dime museum. Never take any more drinks in the early part of the day than are absolutely necessary to brace you up. Three cocktails as eye-openers, followed by two in the way of appetizers, ought to straighten you up before breakfast, and, if not already a slave to tippling, a dozen beers or so ought to satisfy you between then and noon. If tempted to overdo the matter, recall the wax group of the Drunkard's Family in Barnum's old museum, set the teeth hard, and shut down, shut down!

Never forget to say your prayers before

going to sleep, if it is in accordance with your religious convictions.

Never fail to have convictions of some sort. A man without any is like a cat shelling walnuts. Would you be a nonentity, a dolt, a jackass, or a gentleman of distinction, a man of parts, a power in the land?

VIII.

At Public Entertainments.

NEVER, if escorting one lady or several, scuffle and bandy oaths with ticket-speculators at a theater-entrance. Cultivate an easy *hauteur* of manner.

Never, under like environments, offer to bounce the attendant policeman, boots, blue-coat and buttons, if he will only drop his club. Your ladies may object, if the policeman does not.

Never, upon entering, seize an usher by the throat, rub your coupons into his eyes, and loudly demand your seats or his life. A public entertainment is not a rat-baiting.

Never retain your hat and take off your coat and waistcoat at theater or opera. To shed the tile and retain the garments is in better form.

Never whistle, guffaw or make boisterous comments during the rendition of pathetic scenes. Consistency's a jewel.

Never testify your approbation by prolonged roars, cries of "Hear, hear!" tossing your hat in the air, and making quartz-crushers of your feet. Moderate your transports.

Never express your disapproval by furious catcalls, by pelting the performers with stale eggs, or by vociferated injunctions to "choke 'em off," to "burn the crib,"

or to "run down the rag." A pro-
nounced sibilation, accompanied by
judicious barkings, will answer quite as
well.

Never, even if slowly murdered by the
orchestra, betray your sufferings by
idiotic grimaces, violent contortions and
dismal groans. Remember Talleyrand,
who could have smiled his unconscious-
ness even if stabbed in the back.

Never jocosely shout out " Fire !" if a red-
haired lady should rustle into a seat in
front of you. Incendiarism is the legitimate mission of stump-orators and fire-
bugs.

Never bring your opera-glass to bear like
a siege-gun, with your lips spread open
as over a Barmecides free-lunch. Even

a harsh gritting of the teeth, during the operation, is not in the best taste.

Never hold it for a lady to look through, while adjusting her line of vision by the back of her head, and advising her in a hoarse whisper as to the best method for "gunning" her object. Are you at the opera or the race-course ?

Never loudly discuss politics, divorce suits or ministerial scandals at the theater or at a concert when the performance is going on. If speech is silver and silence golden, discussion at such times is metallic to annoyance.

Never, if compelled to quit the building before the entertainment is finished, pass up the aisle on all fours, to avoid an interruption. Siamese obsequiousness is out of place in well-bred audiences.

Never, at the close, hump your way boorishly through the well-dressed throngs, or expedite an exit by flying leaps over the backs of the seats. Even a break over the stage would be preferable to this form.

Never, after a brief adjournment to the open air, apologize to the lady under your escort with a profuseness that will render the cloves, burned coffee or smoked herring too apparent on your breath. Better confess at once to a gin-sour, and be done with it. Frankness and rankness rhyme but in materiality where truth is at stake.

Never send flowers to the stage in a

market-basket, or bombard a *diva* with bouquets bigger than a cooking-stove. The language of flowers should appeal to the inner sense.

Never enter a crowded auditorium with your thumbs in the arm-holes of your waistcoat, head thrown back, chin in air, and the stub of a cigar between the teeth. Self-consciousness may be pushed to an extreme.

Never lunch between acts, in full view of audience, on cheap sandwiches, peanuts and ginger-beer, even if you have missed your supper. Secretly tighten your waist-band, and think of Baron Trenck and his fortitude in prison.

Never blow your nose with a loud trumpeting during an especially interesting scene, or while a difficult aria is being sung. A fanfare is not necessarily in sympathy with a *tremolo*.

Never, if with a lady, individualize the features of a ballet. A grinning reticence in this regard is more delicate.

Never attempt to join in with the chorus, even at a negro minstrel show. Even burnt-cork has its privileges.

Never permit a lady to pay for the tickets at the box-office. If you havn't any money, don't go.

Never, on seeing a lady home, hint that ice-cream and oyster-saloons are dangerous places at night, the common resorts of tramps, thieves, prize-fighters and penniless adventurers. Veracity is one of the characteristics of high breeding.

Never, if her residence is closed for the night, leave her on the stoop, while you go for a policeman to batter in the door. Ring the bell, and wait.

Never say, in wishing her good-night, that she has cost you a pot of money, but that her society was something of an equivalent. If she really esteems you, she will have inferred as much.

Never criticise her conduct during the evening, even if it may not have come up to your standard. Respect her *amour propre.*

THE END.

A GREAT HIT.

— • • —

A NAUGHTY GIRL'S DIARY

— BY —

AUTHOR OF

"A Bad Boy's Diary."

FULL OF FUN.

Price 50 cents.

Never:

A Hand-Book for the Uninitiated and Inexperienced Aspirants to Refined Society's Giddy Heights and Glittering Attainments.

www.ingramcontent.com/pod-product-compliance
Lightning Source LLC
Chambersburg PA
CBHW032203010726
47493CB00008BA/2810